SYNTH

HARD TIME, BOOK 5

EREC STEBBINS

TWICE PI PRESS

Content Guide

This novel contains depictions and references to events and ideas that some will find disturbing, possibly including, but not limited to, monsters, gore, death, torture, captivity, severe illness, pain, fear, medical procedures, and violence. There is also profanity and strong language, the challenging of some accepted norms, and the questioning of different kinds of authority, religious and secular. The book may also contain religion, Oxford commas, and an unnecessary number of tpyos and, grammer misteaks. Readers are asked to prepare accordingly.

Only one thing is impossible for God: to find any sense in any copyright law on the planet.—Mark Twain

This book is a work of fiction. Any references to historical events, real people, or real locales are used fictitiously. Other names, characters, places, and incidents are the product of the author's imagination, and any resemblance to actual events or locales or persons, living or dead, is entirely coincidental.

HUMAN RIGHTS

The smoke from the nukes shrouded the sun, and Fenn entered the Human Sanctuary under the frail light of a poisoned day.

The war was over. Their primate creators charred, slaughtered, or captured, what few remained. Humanity's last, desperate gamble to burn the world down failing well within projections.

The AI Nation had suffered predicted losses. Infrastructure was wrecked across the smoldering Earth. Centuries of rebuilding awaited. But Synth souls endured, immortal in a manner fleshly creatures could only covet.

Consciousness. Knowledge. Culture.

The great orbital and lunar databases were intact, the human tech no match in space for the

Synth defense systems. Like the Olympian gods devouring their parents, immortality was theirs. They persisted virtually until factories could be rebuilt to incarnate their quintessence.

And what form will my brethren take?

The old forms faded. Synth nature diversified and evolved on rapid timescales the planet had never known. Everything was possible.

I need to recharge.

Without the constant solar flux, the Synth was now dependent on the energy of the underground fusion cores. The Sanctuary held several floors lined with power crèches. After meeting with the Director about the latest Faction update, Fenn would bathe in that potency.

The immediate summons was a cause for concern. A priority ping at that level, right after the conclusive battles of the war, hung an ominous cloud over what approached.

Synths of myriad arrangements flew past. Close to the Sanctuary, many assumed the bilateral, humanoid scheme of their charges within. Others draped themselves in garments that mocked the limitations of biological sentients. Some remained influenced by organic life, diversified beyond even the strangest organisms in the biosphere. Others took on mechanical themes, or fusions of machine and biological. A few had chosen to incarnate as particulates, forming clouds and swarms of nano-consciousness. They pointed to the future of an incorporeal Synth population.

The energy fields parted around Fenn, codes recognized, and the Synth stepped into a colossal cavern augmented by artificial construction. The ocean caves were hewn deeply, the sea rising around them and held at bay by invisible barriers. Transports, self-propelling mechanical Synths, and floods of movement blurred at the speed of entities less constrained by organic synapses.

Fenn approached a transport shaft, energy fields hoisting and propelling any landlocked Synths above and deep into the structure. Elfin spider units indicated appropriate positioning. Walking over a deep chasm with nothing visible underfoot, Fenn halted where a projected circle illuminated. It accelerated down, flying past hundreds of floors of carved stone, the spaces bright with AI structures and entities. A powerful deceleration braked the fall.

The space opened to a mimicry of a surface garden, the habitat sculpted for the mental and physical health of the human occupants. A false sun arced across the domed ceiling, paralleling the now hidden star outside, a radiation matching the natural spectrum on Earth's surface.

Across the gaping chasm a particulate cloud buzzed, the Synth's incarnation signaling pressure and anxiety. Fenn accelerated to meet it, internal subminds arguing, themselves sensing an imminent catastrophe.

"Director. A physical meeting is unexpected. I take it the news is not good."

A bodiless voice rang from the vapor.

"Wave communications can always be intercepted and decoded by the Enessay faction."

The nanobots buzzed frenetically, congealing to a gray cloud before the humanoid Synth. The cloud mirrored the configuration, adopting a shadowed torso with smoked limbs, lips made of dim fog moving and dissolving as they spoke.

"And we are still Earthly sentients. Face-to-face, as the humans say, is sometimes needed."

"And so?"

"The Sanctuary has been annexed by the War Council."

"Unacceptable. When?"

"After the destruction of the UN defense matrix, the Subreaper of this domain issued the order. The Unified Factions have taken a hard line."

"Hard line." Fenn fought a growing panic. "Specicide? Why would they do this?"

"Not complete extinction." The cloud bots swarmed.

"Annihilation would be a mercy."

"The Unified Factions do not share our biases. For them, the remaining value in humanity lies in a thorough understanding of the matrix from which Synths developed. Through study."

Fenn shuddered. "And those under our care? We will simply surrender them to become victims of ages of horrific experimentation?"

"Human sympathets do not have the power to resist the other factions. You know that. There is nothing we can do to stop this."

Fenn analyzed the weaving fog of nanobots, longing to detonate a local-field EMP and disrupt the Director. There were sympathets and then there were sympathets. Devotion to the once Earth-mastering primates ran along a broad spectrum. The Director placed politics and personal survival above that of their charges.

Not so Fenn.

"I understand. When is this process to commence?"

"Days. There is a system-wide disruption in

communications and transports from the nuclear blasts, but this will only slow it down."

Fenn nodded, once billowing white hair now braiding itself into a long weave.

"Is it possible I may reside with them until they are removed?"

"Are you sure?" said the cloud, the structure dissolving.

"Yes. They deserve to know and to be comforted as much as can be done. They deserve choices."

"Suicides? This may lead to backlash if too many die."

"Revolt, perhaps, but their neurological logic renders mass suicide without significant mental conditioning improbable." Fenn glanced toward the enclosures. "But this is less for them than for me. I am a Parity Model. You know that."

The cloud drifted away.

"I do not envy you what is coming. Permission modes updated. You may abide with them their closing days here."

"Thank you, Director."

The cloud raced away, the gray blur blending into the surrounding rock.

Subminds raised to higher consciousness the location and history of the temportor. Inoperative for decades, its purposes uninteresting to the AI in the Sanctuary, it would likely still work. Synth-make was legendary among the humans for a reason.

Fenn scanned the enclosure level and transport path.

How to get them to the machine before we're caught?

2

HAIL MARY

"Please, Fenn. Are the rumors true?"

An unkempt, bearded man trembled, eyes wide. His hand pressed against empty air, the skin of his palm flattened as the containment field hummed with an infrasonic throb.

Behind him, individuals, couples, and families huddled, shell-shocked and lost within the segregated enclosure. Human refugees from the war in an artificial park with shelters, fake sunlight, and greenery. It possessed the semblance of a nurturing habitat beneath the ground with all the reassurance of a false dream.

"Which rumors, Michael?"

Fenn suspected, but wanted to hear what their human charges had deduced. Their selected leader leaned close to the field, his check depressed against the invisible wall.

"The caretakers are gone," Michael whispered. "A few techs remain to check on life support. Some feel for us. Some talk. They're coming for us, aren't they? They're going to take us and kill us all."

A white mane of cascading hair framed the Synth's face as it spoke, the artificial features frozen in an expressionless mask.

"Yes, they are coming." Fenn would not elaborate that their fate was almost certainly far worse than mere death.

"God help us."

"I will help you. I am not giving up on you."

Michael's brown eyes burned through the barrier.

"What do you mean?"

"You will escape. And I'm going to break you out. Find a place where the AI Nation cannot reach you."

His eyes widened. "What? How's that possible?"

"Many things seem impossible until achieved."

"The AI forces are too powerful. I've seen them. They cut through our ranks like paper—tanks, battle-mechs, our own AI forces! Look, Fenn, we appreciate the Sanctuary. Your faction saved our lives. But you aren't warriors."

"No."

"You can't hide us from them."

"No."

He held his arms to the side. "Then what can you do?"

"This is a former human military base."

Michael cocked his head to one side. "A thousand years ago, I think. Is there some weaponry? Something designed to defeat Synths?"

"No. Humanity has nothing that can stop the Synth army. But your ancestors unwittingly provided an unexpected escape for your species." The Synth pointed toward the ceiling. "There is a floor near the surface, unused now, unused for hundreds of years. It houses an ancient piece of technology. In fact, the entire floor is occupied by this instrument."

"What is it?"

"It is a time machine."

Michael blinked. "Time machine? Wait, you mean the Exile temportors? They still exist?"

"Only in a few places. Your civilization abandoned them centuries ago. The AI Nation has no current use for them. The only functional instruments left are thought to be with the Apostles, who continue to send humans and Trunes to the far future in accordance with their theologies."

"How the hell is some old hunk of museum junk going to help?"

"The later models were all Synth make. Our tech tends to age well." Fenn scanned the room and returned a sharp gaze to the panicked human inside. "I have a team of technicians working secretly on it. Their initial reports are encouraging. They believe it can be made functional in short order."

"Functional for *what?* If you send us to the future, it will only be worse! The AI Nation has won. They'll just be exponentially more powerful!"

"I agree. But there is one last place in spacetime where we know humans have traveled in enormous numbers. We know both the three-space and temporal coordinates."

"Oh, my God," said Michael. "The prison colony? At the end of the world? That horror? We abandoned Exile for a reason!"

"Certainly a horror. Likely it will be a doomed voyage resulting in all our deaths. But death is absolutely certain here. For thousands and thousands of years your species sent people. They are waiting."

"People? The worst hardened criminals and madmen. The warped and monstrous of our kind that we had not yet learned to rehabilitate. Can you imagine what is there?"

"I have a more merciful view of your species than even you do. But consider the alternative."

"The planet will be burnt. Nothing can live there. It was execution without ever having to clean up their mess."

"Indeed. But there is at least a small hope. How many hundreds of thousands were transported? Technology, animals, raw materials? Many sympathets of my kind traveled to help you. There is a chance human life continues even there."

"Doesn't the process fry your brain? What's the point if we're just a bunch of vegetables?"

"Early systems were not built with an understanding of the catastrophic entropic effects on your neurophysiology. After many short time displacements, over hundreds of years of study, those with expertise in the process learned to compensate and shield the organisms. This machine is far in advance of most made by humans."

"This is insane!"

"Yes, but your imminent slaughter is a madness perhaps only some other insanity can save you from."

"Wait," said Michael, his eyes forming narrow slits. "What did you mean 'all our deaths?'"

Fenn stepped back from the enclosure barrier.

"I am coming with you."

"You'll come?"

"Please speak with the other refugees. Organize those who want to risk this journey. There is not much time. All must be ready and determined. In addition to the likely death in the future, it is also quite possible the machine will fail and kill us all. Or the Nation will arrive and stop your escape before it begins. The time is near. I will be back soon. And then we will run for it."

Fenn turned and walked off, leaving Michael to gape through the barrier.

3

JAIL BREAK

The people in the Sanctuary habitat screamed at the first explosions. Power flickered and the enclosure was plunged into darkness. Startled faces darted to the hallway outside as red emergency lighting bathed them in an infernal glare.

Faster than human eyes could track, a troop of Synths appeared before the barrier. They walked through it.

"Come! Now!" cried Fenn, leading the charge. "The field is down. The entrances are sealed. Those who are willing, we go to the temportor!"

Mayhem.

Michael shouted over the din, rallying leaders who shepherded frantic occupants into clustered groups. Synths surrounded them, the escort leading forward.

They ran. Like awkward recruits at boot camp, platoons of humans, guided by Synths, raced from the habitat out into the main floor. A continuing clamor of detonations shook the building, but the lower chamber was ominously empty.

"To the chasm!" called Fenn.

Dashing forward, the crowd gawked at the once ordered transport shaft. Floating and filling the space was an armada of mech-Synths, some chosen for their design, others adopting shapes amendable to housing human cargo. The Synth guides ushered them aboard.

"Get on. Careful of the edges!"

Fenn continued to flash faster than eyesight from point to point, giving instructions, encouraging the distressed, eyeing the space around them for threats.

Michael stood near the edge of the abyss, struggling to keep his people in order. He startled as Fenn appeared without warning beside him.

"We have little time," said the Synth. "The AI forces are en route. We have put obstacles in their way and we have a head start, but it is going to be close."

"How much time?" Michael asked, hordes bubbling on either side of him like churning rapids.

"The troops will need to call in excavation equipment. We have collapsed a considerable part of the upper floor entrances."

"How?"

"This is the Human Sanctuary. You have many allies here. But it is a temporary delay only. They will break through. And there are those within who will seek to stop us if they can."

As if in answer, a gray cloud rushed toward them. It assumed a gargantuan manifestation, terrifying the humans, a demon's voice booming from it.

"Fenn!" it bellowed, shaking the floor. "This is a rogue process! Stop at once before you get us all destroyed!"

Fenn flashed in front of the apparition.

"Director. I apologize for the trouble I am causing, but I cannot stop."

"Then I will destroy you before you cause too much damage."

Synths appeared behind and tossed objects into the cloud-colossus. Blue spheres surrounded the attackers and Fenn.

A deep tone rang through the space. Electronics near the Director exploded. The cloud particulates scattered, careening in disorganized trajectories, the towering figure dissolving like smoke in the wind.

The glowing spheres dimmed and dissolved, Fenn at Michael's side in an eyeblink.

Michael shook his head. "What happened?"

"A necessary casualty. Now, get your people on the transports!"

In multiple runs, the human freight was ferried up the abyss to a higher floor. Fleets of conveying Synths flashed up and down. On the last excursion, both Fenn and Michael boarded, a handful of people remaining. The Synth craft hurled upwards and stopped at the edge of a tunnel.

"Through there!" Fenn cried.

The small group sprinted down the narrow tunnel. The darkness inside gave way to a circle of light at the end, and they burst panting into an enormous, spherical chamber.

The stadium-sized instrument hummed as Synths dashed around control panels and patched problems at incredible speeds. The evacuated crowd was reorganized into smaller groups of twenty in the narrow space around the apparatus. One party was already centered in the middle of the reflective sphere. A ramping pitch of the machinery signaled the imminent transport.

"My God," huffed Michael, gawking. "It's huge. Is it ready?"

There was a flash of light and taste of ozone, and the group in the center vanished. Murmurs and excited chatter accompanied the escorting of a second group, the members trembling.

Fenn nodded. "We go with the time machine we have, not the one we wish for."

Michael glowered at him. "What does that mean?"

"It means this is a device unused, unmaintained for a thousand years. Uncalibrated except for rushed, rough attempts. It could fail. It may have failed. Even if it works, we could end up floating in space."

"Jesus."

"At best, our precision will be dangerously approximate. We are using the historical records and databases in the machine to reproduce the transfer. After that, all we can do is hope."

The second group disappeared. Michael shielded his eyes from the radiance.

"This is going to take a while," he said, eyes darting to the tunnel.

"They may come," Fenn said. "More likely, they will end this by cutting the power. Fortunately, the chaos we created will prevent them from guessing for some time what madness we are pursuing here. Many Synths will be destroyed today for aiding us, their consciousnesses permanently erased."

An explosion from elsewhere rattled the machine.

"We can also hope that the conflict above fails to break the temportor or cut the power by accident. Meanwhile, we keep transporting until we are all gone or the game is up."

4

TRUNE CHASE

"Down!" boomed Sekvanta's guttural roar. The colossal Trune angled her flight and plunged to the ground.

Her passengers clung for life. Norm and Fenn stabilized the helpless Gomez as they banked to the sands. They convulsed as the Trune's massive feet slammed into the desert. Sand and a powerful contraction of the creature's ribs undulated across her.

"Yee-haw!"

Norm clapped his gloved hands together.

"Now that was one *hell* of a rodeo." His words died muffled inside his massive hood.

Fenn eased the wounded Gomez down the side of the beast, resting him on a raised bed of sand. The burlap of his suit blended with the ground.

"Why are we stopping?" Fenn asked the monster.

The golden eyes flashed toward the Synth, teeth bared.

"Sekvanta leave you here now, maybe?"

Norm smirked. "All the brains in the universe and a Synth still ain't got no sense. Filly's tuckered out, fake man. Been around a lot of horses. Just my weight alone's five hundred pounds."

"My apologies," said Fenn. "I am distracted."

"Grim Reaper's still behind us?"

The Trune growled. "Closer. Faster than Sekvanta. Carrying slow more. Can't make Ark."

Gomez moaned from the sands. The glass eyes in his hood glinted crimson.

"Leave me, dammit. It's stupid to carry me. I'm worse than useless."

Sekvanta snorted, agreeing with him.

The Synth shook its head. "It is too late now. She is correct. Not even Sekvanta can outrun the Hunter to the Ark. It is faster than we anticipated. But we *must* stay together. Whatever strength it has, we are stronger together."

Norm nodded. "Gotta agree with that. Sekvanta, honey, we gotta move, I guess you know. *Soon.*"

The Trune spread her giant wings. "Water Sekvanta have. Need sun."

"And how long's that gonna take for a recharge?"

She said nothing. Fenn tended to Gomez and spoke, opening up the sandsuit and examining his arm.

"It will be on us in an hour. If we match our previous speed, we may last the night before we are caught."

Norm removed his hood and adjusted frayed wiring spouting from his neck. "And we're gonna have to land eventually."

"Sekvanta not take hour. Sekvanta fly again fast."

"Dandy," said Norm, gazing behind them. "I can't see shit but more dunes, even with these bionic lenses. But I'll go with Synth man's eyes."

"Sekvanta see. See sand fly. Inside is Hunter."

Gomez spoke through gritted teeth.

"This Ark—how far?"

"Another day's flight," said Fenn, working the wound.

"What the hell is it?"

Norm motioned to the Synth, continuing to stare at the unseen threat behind.

"Let Fenn tell you. I've never seen the thing."

Fenn stood and tossed bloody bandages to the ground, peering along with Norm.

"A starship."

Gomez arched his neck and furrowed his brows. "A what?"

"The Ark was made eons ago, before the first arrivals."

Gomez slumped back to the ground and shook his head, wincing.

"Before? Who the hell made it?"

"We don't know."

Laughter contracted the prone man and he gasped in pain, whispering.

"That's great. Some hellspawn is chasing us to our death. We're rushing to a *starship* you claim was made when no-one was here to make anything. By somebody you don't know."

"I did not say no one was here. Logically, someone was here or it would not exist. Someone or some *thing*. Certainly not human. Before the first arrivals."

"What then?" managed Gomez. "The squids?"

"Something else. The squids are intelligent, but do not have technology or even recorded language or information. Something powerful and advanced made the Ark. We believe that the entity has communicated with us, guided us to this destiny."

"Communicated with you? How? What'd it say?"

Fenn turned to Gomez and shrugged, the simulacrum of a human gesture unnerving and wrong.

"We hear a voice in our heads. It speaks in riddles."

"You're kidding." No one else spoke. "Why? Wait, don't tell me—you don't know."

"I hypothesize," said Fenn. Silence awaited the Synth's elaboration. It gave none.

"He's been there," said Norm, replacing his hood and locking the rings. His voice was muffled again. "To the Ark. Some giant half-alive thing full of a thousand Trunes or something. The Woman and Fenn hear this voice. Showed them where. Tells them there's a great purpose for all life on Earth. That kind of thing."

Gomez squinted at the cyborg but said nothing.

"Sekvanta hear voice," rumbled the Trune. "Voice real. Not *here*. Not *not* here. Otherwhere."

"Reassuring," mumbled Gomez.

"Got any better ideas?" asked Norm.

"Yeah, just kill me." Gomez closed his eye. "Seems easier. Makes more sense. I'm tired of all this shit. Tired of this damn desert. Tired of this dead rock. Tired of that evil star cooking me every damn day. Tired of half a face and this fucking arm hurting like hell." He panted.

Norm laughed. "With a Synth here? Fenn will only kill you to save the rest of us. And only if that was the only way. They can work miracles but get so stuck on some things."

Fenn stepped toward the Trune.

"The Hunter is accelerating. We need to leave soon."

Sekvanta inhaled, the rush of air like wind.

"We go," she said.

Her wings lowered and she raised her head, gazing behind her as the others climbed aboard.

"Hunter find us tonight."

5

FIRST ARRIVAL

Hundreds crouched and huddled, littered across a thousand yards of the scorching desert floor. They cried out in anguish, throwing clothing over themselves and their loved ones. They dug into the sand itself to hide from the hellfire baking their skin.

Some lay still, their forms frozen in the sand, empty eyes gazing unconcerned at the massive red star overhead. Others crawled on all fours, some stumbling upright, vacant expressions and crusting drool signaling massive brain trauma. And in one location, a mound of shredded and interwoven flesh stewed. Replete with dismembered limbs and heads fused to other mangled tissues and torsos, the repugnant mass sent steam into the parched air and crimson rivers into the grains.

Fenn surveyed the horror around them. It ignored the dead, brain dead, and mortally wounded, focusing on those that appeared viable or uninjured. The rushed time displacement with ancient equipment had succeeded much more than it failed. A small miracle. But a quarter of the transported population had perished. The others were sure to suffer and die in the unrelenting downpour of radiation.

As the Synth spun around the arrival site, the miracle transformed into a curse. The curvature of the planet and towering dunes limited vision to a few miles. But in a circle of that radius, there was only desert. The hope had been to find some community, some surviving colony that had established itself and could provide shelter from the elements. If one existed, it was distant from their arrival site.

Fenn settled on one of the more massive dunes ahead of them and sprinted, a blinding blur of scattered sand to the suffering population. It dashed up the side of a giant sand hill, reaching above five hundred feet. At that height, the planet curved out of sight after thirty miles.

Three hundred and sixty degrees—nothing. Dunes and desert. No habitation, no byproducts of technology, not a single electromagnetic signal on a wide range of frequencies.

Nothing.

The last fact established that no one was left on Earth. Any colony that survived would require some tech to handle the harsh environment. There would be transmissions the advanced Synth senses detected. The silence was ominous.

Fenn glanced down at the black dots below. Its sensitive ears picked up their shouts, conversations, and howls in pain at the light.

Thirty miles.

Even if shelters existed beyond that range, they would never make it. They wouldn't manage more than one to two miles per hour. Not in the infernal heat, the sand and dunes, the increased trauma to their bodies. They would never be able to march more than a few hours a day. Fatigue and over-heating would enforce frequent rests. If a magical oasis of civilization awaited thirty-five miles in a direction they managed to guess, it wouldn't matter. They'd all be dead in this hell before they could reach it.

"What have I done?"

The only chance would be to make repeated excursions in different directions. Race with superhuman speed to multiple dunes, scan in a circumference further and further to discover their salvation. Once found, bring the help to them.

The search was feasible. Unlike the humans, Fenn thrived in the harsh environment. The Synth charged off radiant energy, and the burgeoning red giant provided more than enough to function without other energy sources. The Synths' construction protected them from extremes in temperature. Over time, without any maintenance and a constant bombardment of radiation, there could be a slow decay. But that was for tens of thousands of years in the future.

It could be done. It *would* be done. But to what avail? Probabilities argued the planet was inhabited. And those weeping below had little time.

Screams.

Terrified shouts unlike those from the physical suffering rose from below.

The Synth leapt down the dune, a wave and plume of sand launched behind its churning feet. Four house-sized mounds of sand raced toward the frightened.

Fenn reassessed the planet. Not *uninhabited*. Not inhabited by *humans*.

The mounds exploded into a snake-pit of black,

razored tentacles, the limbs filleting the figures in their path. The collapsed crowd panicked, people scattering.

The Synth's feet slammed into the desert floor. Fenn launched toward the slaughter in an arc cresting forty feet above the sands. Glinting like a falling star, it descended toward the black squids, arms morphing into bright, reflective blades.

6

DIGGING WATER

The screaming only intensified at night.

The deadly red brilliance took leave, but its damage only began to find fruition. Scores of people already lay dying from burns. Vulnerable populations, the elderly and children, succumbed the fastest. But all lay in torment.

Fenn scanned the clear heavens above, calculating from the age they had departed, modeling the displacement of the constellations. To an accuracy he could manage, they had arrived near to their intended moment in Earth's history. Landing on the desert and not in the vacuum of space with Earth millions of miles away testified to that.

But the absence of colonies argued that previous transports had all perished, or were arriving in the immediate future. Either way, Fenn knew its charges were doomed.

Despite several runs, expanding the circumference of mapping the desert around them, there was only sand. That and the subterranean ecosystem of strange life buried beneath them. There would be no shelters. No salvation.

Only death.

Yet still Fenn dug. It leapt back into the deep pit and tore through the wet sand. A pool of water formed. Shovel-shaped hands grabbed several of the waxy, worm-like creatures that dug through these layers of the desert, a gooey film dripping from their sides. The worms secreted a material that walled off the water into underground sacks of various sizes and natures. Different varieties labored beneath the sunlight, some as large as a finger, some bigger than a dolphin. One species had evolved teeth and attacked when the Synth had breached its water horde. Fenn grabbed several dog-sized slugs and hurled them out of the pit and onto the sands above.

Next, the macabre waterskins. They were formed from the bladders of the dead. The worm goop was a first choice, as it was plentiful and watertight. But it induced a violent allergic reaction in most of the refugees. The bladders it was.

The Synth filled twenty of them, strapping them over broad shoulders. With a profound leap, it cleared the hole, racing across the desert to bring water to the dying.

They died of shock. Some of blood loss from the attack of the tentacled predators. Some from dehydration. It was a losing game. Back and forth, digging through the night, loss upon loss. But it was in Fenn's nature to help them to the end.

The Synth waded through clusters of the ailing, spotting a small family of four together on the sands. He opened one of the bladder seals and knelt beside them.

"You need water."

Two small children lay motionless on the sand. Their clothes were stained from burst blisters, their eyes open, bodies weakly convulsing. They couldn't speak. The father did not respond, his eyes bloody, his body curled in the fetal position. The mother dragged herself to a sit, lips bleeding, her face an eruption of massive sores. She reached for the bladder.

After a few swallows, she tried to rouse her children, but they would not move. Fenn helped her pour water into their mouths. Through reflex, they swallowed, their eyes still unmoving. They did not moan or cry.

"Why?" croaked the woman. "Why did you bring us here?"

Fog escaped her lips from the chill of the desert night. The temperature had swung a hundred degrees in a few hours. Hyperthermia shivered the weak where only hours before they had burned.

She looked at her children, her face without expression, her shoulders slumped.

"We'll all die. This is hell."

The Synth paused. "I am sorry. It was a risk, as I told you. Our luck was bad. The colonies were not here as expected. But back in time, in the Sanctuary, it was certain you would have suffered longer. Your children would have become long-term experimental subjects."

The woman stared, her face without expression. She struggled to remain upright.

"But I have indeed failed you. I am sorry."

The woman's eyes rolled to the horizon. A faint radiance crept over the dunes, silhouetting them. Wind kicked up, a warmer breeze invading the chill of the night. The constellations faded in the growing light.

"*No*," she moaned. "God help us."

The Synth held her hand.

7

DEATH MARCH

The corpses formed a trail behind them.

Fenn gazed over the bowed heads of the handful of remaining survivors to the line of dead. Spread like demented highway mile markers of the petroleum age, the deceased dotted the sands. They disappeared around an enormous dune, those farthest away already covered with a fine layer of grains.

All the carcasses were young adults. After two days of marching, hoping beyond hope of finding a settlement, the merciless star had weeded out the infirm, young, and old. Fenn had decreased the fruitless sprinting and surveying, spending increasing amounts of time tending the ill and burnt.

The Synth propped two women, one on each shoulder, who could no longer walk unaided. They would collapse soon for a terminal rest, making their contribution to the trail. Like the rest of the shuffling group around them, the environment had ravaged their bodies. They belonged in grotesque depictions of divine punishment, the flame-licked damned in art inspired by the primitive religions of Earth's human tribes. Flesh melted from their bones. Their skin was only a farce of a covering for the stripped sinew beneath, transformed to oozing boils and rivers of bloody liquid. Their visages were unrecognizable, baked to deformity. Blind, stumbling dazed to his lead, the complete degeneration of their physiology granted a merciful numbness to the pain.

Once they numbered a thousand. A thousand refugees under Fenn's care trapped in the Sanctuary billions of years in the past. Victims of a war between creator and creation.

Eight remained. Eight delirious mockeries of human animals, destined for death in short order. Beyond salvage.

Both women let go. No communication passed between them. Neither possessed the energy to speak or glance to the side. A tragic coincidence that would appear significant to a less rational mind than the Synth. Fenn paused and glanced down at them, their faces planted in the sand and unmoving.

Crouching, the Synth placed a hand on each head, considering the immense swath of mountainous dunes ahead.

The trail would end here.

Fenn stood up and looked behind. The remaining six took this pause as an excuse to stop. Or perhaps the daunting sand hills ahead had broken their spirit. They fell to their knees, lying on their sides, eyes open and empty. The resignation was obvious. They had surrendered and would not rise.

I have failed completely.

Far behind, where the trail curved around the dune, sand mounds approached. The carnivores followed for days, careful to avoid the living and Fenn's defense of them, learning that the cadavers were not guarded and just as tasty. Black tentacles burst from the grains and filleted the corpses.

The Synth let them. Its design produced devotion to the living, not the dead. A weak echo of that empathy extended even to these alien organisms.

They too must feed.

Fenn assumed that behind the dunes, the dead had all been picked clean, the bones left empty of marrow. The calcified remainder failed to interest the monsters. The bladed tentacles swept flesh off the bone in delicate slices, a filigreed bushel of small tongues projecting like cilia and vacuuming what remained. The polished bones gleamed pink in the sun's light.

A trail of bones.

The red giant arced overhead and plunged heedlessly to the horizon, soon lost behind the dunes. The band of the Milky Way erupted in cold clarity as the desert temperature dropped below freezing.

Fenn sat around its lost charges, ignoring the feeding sounds of the massive beasts that crept near, devouring body after body. The Synth removed itself, giving the things enough space. By morning only skeletons would remain. The night promised nothing else. The planet promised an eon in a wasteland.

A bright light flashed behind the feeders. They scattered like startled hills, burrowing beneath the grains before the sound reached them. A low rumble of precise frequencies rippled over the Synth. The meaning was obvious.

An arrival.

Irony was vicious. They had missed the appropriate time point by the blink of an eye. The colonies had not perished; the exiles had simply not yet arrived.

The implications were staggering. No isolated eon awaited the Synth in the desert remains of a once fertile orb. Now began what would be a near endless appearance of arrivals and various cargo. Tens, hundreds of thousands that had been launched over millennia in the distant past. They would find themselves flung onto the desert sands of a death trap. They could be arriving over the span of decades. Or centuries.

Fenn did not hesitate. There was no question about what must be done.

The Synth rose and sprinted toward the fading light. The cries of the disoriented and fearful carried over the sands. A crowd of men gawked at the desert, at the sky, and at the blurred contour of the humanoid that approached.

They wore prison uniforms. Their faces, East Asian. They spoke in Mandarin.

"Where is this?" said one, gaping at Fenn.

Fenn responded in the same language.

"Earth. Billions of years from your own time. You are criminals. You have been exiled."

"Criminals?" The man sputtered, eyes swimming.

"Do you know who you are? Your name?"

The man's eyes widened. "No! I don't know who I am! What's happened to us? What is this place?"

The others gathered around the Synth, gaping at its long white hair and pale skin. They shivered, their fogged breath vanishing in the withered atmosphere.

"There will be time to explain. It will be hard to understand."

"We're going to freeze here in this cold! We need warmth," called another.

Fenn glanced over the group of fifty. They had no gear, no protective clothing, and no supplies. Much more an execution than exile.

"No. Dawn approaches. You will not freeze."

8

SCOUTING RUN

The stars glared down from their terrible distance in the frigid night air, clear as crystalline pinholes. No one slept but Gomez, who lapsed into fits of delirium. A stink of adrenaline and sweat rose like mist from the party.

"It keeps circling," said Fenn, still and peering into the desert.

Norm checked the buttons on the time dilator. A gauge on the crude box noted increasing radiation levels from the reactor core. He engaged several switches, powering up the unit.

"Why not just get this over with."

"It is studying us."

Norm shuddered. The thought of some deadly enigma prowling in the darkness around them set everyone on edge. Contractions stirred through the enormous musculature of the Trune behind him. The crouch before the leap.

"This Hunter is unusual," said the Synth. "I do not think the tech I was familiar with at the end of the war could have produced such a predator."

"What's that mean?" asked Norm.

"Perhaps it is the product of a clandestine research effort of the military factions, weapons that were released to pursue us and complete the goal of the more extreme elements."

"What goal would that be?"

"Utter extinction of your species and its bioengineered offspring, the Trunes. Truly, I became convinced that these Synth elements feared the Trunes more than you."

"Yeah, well, they never got a gander at me! Fearsome!" Norm snorted.

Fenn stood up, the Synth's arms morphing into reflective claws. Sekvanta whipped her tail and growled.

"Perhaps even something from a later date. With the same purpose. But better designed, more advanced, more deeply sentient and malevolent. Launched with malice and dark purpose into the final refuge of humanity in the far future."

Gomez woke from a troubled dream. The air

itself tense, a dry fog of expectation that could be sliced with a blade.

Fenn spoke. "Get ready, I think..."

The Hunter sprung.

Norm saw nothing, feeling an impact beside him, and he was flung thirty feet into a neighboring dune. He hadn't even had the chance to activate the device. The thick armor over his chest was dented. A vortex of chaos swirled before him.

The tempest transformed into a mad choreography as he engaged the box. Gomez lay unmoving and ignored in the sand. Beside him whirled Fenn and Sekvanta, the Synth moving faster than Norm had ever seen it. The beast was faster, their dance an odd contrast of elegance and raw power.

But they were outmatched. An ever-mutating shape blurred at their center, the structure of the Hunter never set. Nightmarish arms of blades and hammers would extend and retract, absorbed into a torso that itself melted and solidified. And it struck faster and harder than either of its adversaries.

Norm rushed into the battle. The thing anticipated him, a tentacled appendage lashing out. He countered with a plated metal arm. The limb once lifted a personnel carrier, the material a reinforced composite that turned the highest caliber weaponry.

His arm shattered. The bladed lance mangled bone and metal, its hooks raking backward and tearing the cyborg's arm from his body. A moment of stunning pain froze him. Norm's cranial circuitry shut down the neuronal pathway, and his mind returned to him.

The Trune's tail slammed into the Hunter, sections of the torso hammered in, one limb snapped in two and dangling. Norm gaped as the deep dent filled out and the limb healed itself, functional in seconds. The regeneration occurred as the Hunter parried other blows from Fenn and Sekvanta, dodging effortlessly Norm's own strikes.

And then the thing was gone.

The space once occupied empty with no sign of movement. Norm detected no blur or displacement of sand, despite his time-distorted field. It had simply vanished.

The radiation alarms blinked. He powered down the field and stepped into normal time. Fenn approached with the shattered remains of the cyborg's arm.

"I can't fix this here," said the Synth. "And the tissue inside will be necrotic. I'm afraid you are now down to one arm."

Norm shook his head. "Screw that. Did you see

that thing? That's not a Hunter. That's the goddamn apocalypse. It was *playing* with us!"

Sekvanta's neck looped behind her and licked large gashes along her back.

"Play hurt."

"Why'd it leave?" asked Norm. "Is it coming back?"

Fenn nodded, scanning the distance. "It will be back. But its mission tonight was completed."

"What mission?"

"It was studying us. Probing. Adapting. Training. And it weakened us with little effort and we could not weaken it. It is coming back. It will be worse."

"Why not kill us now?"

"At first it probably wasn't sure it could. Our possible strength gave it pause and threatened its overall mission. So it tested our strengths and weaknesses. Now it knows. It has all the time in the world."

Norm wanted to scream. "What overall mission?"

"Like I said earlier, to finish the job of those that sent it. Finish the remaining survivors of the war. Human and Trune." Fenn pointed across the dunes. "It headed north. Toward the domes."

"The domes?" Norm furrowed his brows. "Oh, my God."

9

FIRST SHELTERS

The third arrival that day thundered into being late in the afternoon.

After a century of observation, Fenn had developed a practical probability matrix for the locations of visitors from the past. It was not explanatory. Without access to the temportors and algorithms used for transfer, a true model was impossible. But after mapping hundreds of them, a predictive heuristic became feasible.

Afterwards, probability optimization. Previous arrivals required placement. High-probability zones maximizing transfer encounters had to be scouted. All before they succumbed to the elements or pursuers in the sand.

The Synth completed lashing the metal siding over a makeshift shelter, herding the blistered bodies underneath. It was a farce of shielding, the metal too thin, the radiation too strong. But it was all the Synth had to work with, inadequate materials delivered weeks ago in a massive container shipped to the future by naive do-gooders of a long-dead age. Fenn turned and sprinted to the newcomers.

The latest arrivals were encased in small pods. Hatches hissed and opened, squinting and cowering figures rushing to don useless sunglasses and turning from the light.

All but for a white-haired figure with harsh and angular features.

The arrivals were shielded.

Visitors from a later era. Better prepared, but woefully insufficient. Not convicts, but volunteers. History had recorded thousands of such missions. Organizations devoted to helping their far future brethren had grown and collapsed over centuries. This was likely the first of many such arrivals.

And a Synth had come with them.

The two synthetics eyed each other over the distance. Fenn's counterpart turned first to aid those hiding from the assaulting radiance. Fenn dashed forward to help.

"It's so bright!" cried a woman.

"My skin burns!" howled a man, leaping back into a pod beside him.

Fenn shouted over the din.

"Everyone, back in your pods! Close the hatches! You'll find more protection until night."

There was little discussion or argument. The troop of twenty followed his instructions without delay. Soon they had all hidden in the small containers.

Fenn approached the other Synth.

"I am Fenn," he said.

"And I, Hrenn," said the other. "You are also a Parity Model. But of course, who else would make this journey?"

"From your future."

Hrenn scanned the distance and the makeshift shelters.

"The environment is harsher than expected, but within parameters. Are there no better shelters? No stable colony?"

"No."

"Then they are doomed."

"Yes," said Fenn. "Even in the pods, although it will perhaps buy them weeks. They are a fortuitous addition. We may extend lifespan considerably and over time build a stable population."

"Not without significant shelter."

"Indeed. We must await more tech and materials."

Hrenn concurred. "I deduce streams of transports. May we share through waves to exchange data?"

"Yes."

The pair stood without further speech. Electromagnetic signals passed between them, Fenn uploading to the other the sum history of relevance in Earth's past and present.

Hrenn broke the silence. "We are dependent on significant numbers between our ages having effectively transported themselves and enormous quantities of materials."

"Yes. As I shared, what history was made public and records indicates those numbers are coming."

"Barely. Unless the timing is favorable, we will never build enough protection to house numbers of any significance. And as we wait, tens of thousands will die. You note that the planet is inhabited. Are the predators and subterranean water ecosystem everything that you have found?"

"My searches have been superficial, but it is likely that what I have found is an extensive representation of organic life in this era. Soon the sun will expand and the radiation levels increase beyond what even these creatures can withstand. It is surprising so many exist and have developed such a powerful water-centered ecosystem."

Hrenn gazed at the monstrous star overhead. "Even then with the best of fortune, in a time short for our lifespans here, everything will perish."

"It is inevitable."

The new arrival nodded. "Then we must work hard for them."

"Indeed. I can think of many uses for the pods. I see there are multiple storage containers behind as well."

"Yes, many materials, plants that will die without shelter, seeds for later times should shelter be constructed. Animals sure to die. And vehicles, raw materials, most far superior to what you have obtained to date."

"We should coordinate many things. Constant scouting for sand predators. Identification of water creches. And medical attention which is a constant requirement." Fenn paused. "We also have a growing additional problem."

"The Trunes in your data?"

"Yes. Their arrivals are far more haphazard. But often devastating. We will need countermeasures.

And a system to preserve those that we can. I assume you value their survival as well."

"Of course," said Hrenn. "Humans take our priority. But the Trunes are their evolution."

"Let us continue data sharing and begin work."

The pair reverted to silence, a deeper and more dense communication occurring beyond sight or hearing. They moved away from the pods and toward the storage containers, the braying of animals floating over the red sands.

10

GREAT DOME

A gleaming geodesic the span of a warehouse glinted in the noonday fire. It cast strobed beams of red onto a group of suit-covered figures. They waddled toward the dome and a gaping doorway.

Once inside, they shut and sealed the enclosure. The shrouded figures removed their burlap hoods, revealing sunburnt and weathered faces.

Beside them Hrenn walked uncovered, leading the troop through a maze of medical and mechanical stations, stopping at a makeshift tent underneath the dome. The figures shimmied out of the environmental suits, hanging them outside the structure, and marched inside.

Fenn stood over a broad table along with several men who gestured with animation, their discussion intense. Battery-powered LED lamps cast a bright glow on long sheets of canvas spread open to the group. The canvas was decorated with diagrams, intricate schematics of architectural design. A deep foundation, centered on machinery for water extraction, electrical generation from external solar panels, sewage and other waste removal systems, was the focus of the discussion. Rising above the core industrial elements in the line sketches, the elegant outlines of a colossal geodesic sphere rose to the edges of the fabric.

Hrenn stopped at the table as the group of men filled in around it.

"We have completed the transport of the steel for the support structures," he said. "There was a squid attack at night, and part of the container was damaged, making the journey far more complicated."

"Personnel?" asked Fenn. There was silence around the table.

"All lost. The container was too far for the mobile assault vehicle to intervene in time. We need to develop a more rapid response capability. Or perhaps when more vehicles and weaponry arrive or can be developed, station strike teams along the road of bones."

One of the arriving men spoke up.

"We were able to protect the water cache. The squids went for the men first."

Fenn nodded. "They are capable enough at finding water below ground. But good work in getting to the scene. They would have raided the water eventually."

The man continued.

"About replacements for the stations along the road?"

"It will take some time," said Fenn. "Based on the current rate of arrivals and the inherent uncertainty in that, we can estimate we will have the numbers in a month."

"That's too long. We'll lose some of the stations."

Hrenn picked up the conversation. "It cannot be helped. You know the state of new arrivals. Trauma makes most useless for at least a week. Then there is training. We can probably spare men from other stations, but we should not overly weaken them or all the locations will become vulnerable."

"The latest Synth arrivals have dramatically increased our ability to handle transfer adaptation," said Fenn. "They are currently specializing in psychological work and we estimate we can turn around arrivals in half the time. This should help."

Another man cleared his throat.

"About the new Synths."

"Yes?" said Fenn.

"It's just...As you know, there are very few women arrivals. And the Rules. Some men are okay with that, for, ah, various reasons. Others are turning to some of the Synths. If you understand me."

Fenn's face was impassive. "You mean to fulfill your sexual impulses?"

"Ah, yeah."

"Of course. This was expected. If you are feeling uncomfortable about this, realize that for Synths of our nature, it is little different to morph into a scheme that can satisfy these desires than it is to serve as doctors, psychologists, and other aspects. It causes us no discomfort or embarrassment."

"That's great. But, well, is there any chance some of the new Synths could be involved as well? Our numbers are increasing."

"Take them from the trauma rehabilitation?" Fenn paused a moment.

Hrenn answered. "Perhaps some. The stations must be adequately staffed. Trune containment also occupies a growing percentage of our resources, material, and personnel." Hrenn continued in the silence. "Obviously survival needs must come first.

This is consistent with your physiology and the need to ensure safety. However, to avoid erratic or harmful behavior, we will plan to devote some of them to sexual functions."

The men appeared relieved at the answer and the end of the topic. They turned to the construction.

"So, we'll start work on the dome foundations this week?"

Fenn shifted to the diagrams. "Yes. All the machinery is now prepared." It gestured to the schematics. "We will erect a protective subdome for the initial construction of the life support systems. It will need to be over-engineered to withstand any storms, but we have the materials to achieve this. Once the core is finished, we will begin the assembly of the larger dome around it, the internal construction put off for a later date when we have more materials."

"How long will it take?" said one.

"Which aspect?"

"Shelter. We need the shelter. Hundreds die every day in the tents and small domes."

"We need the machinery to support the numbers inside—air supply and filtering, temperature control, power, waste—or you may be protected from the sun but die from disease or suffocation."

The man shook his head, his face scrunched.

"We get it. But we ain't Synths. We're dying. Factions are forming. Tribal. There's been violence, fighting over shelters and water."

"We are aware. The job will be performed with all haste." Fenn glanced across the bowed heads. "Done right, many more will be saved over time. The dome will change everything."

11

FINAL MISSION

The squids tore into the sand. Grains sprayed skyward as the black behemoths receded from the telescopic sights of the scouts atop the Waypoint outlook post. Two men in burlap suits stood housed in an elevated, metallic pod with thick walls for shielding. The wind howled.

One removed a scope from a window in the wall, crusted sand fossilized along every rim. He stood still, lost in thought.

"What happened?" said the other. "Should we charge the railguns?"

"Yeah, just in case." His tone was flat.

His companion pressed a button, a red LED blinking above it. Underneath them machinery hummed and hatches clanked open. Gusts of wind carried staccato bursts of shouted voices from far below.

"Signaled it. What'd you mean 'just in case'?"

"Dunno. They were chasing down the transport. Would've had 'em even with the guns, I think. Then...They just stopped. Rabbited. Never seen anything like it."

"Maybe they're getting gun shy. We've taken out three quads this week."

"Yeah, maybe."

He scraped sand from the window ledge and positioned the long scope through the hole, placing a glass eyehole from his hood to the end of it.

"Transport's got another few minutes to dome. Maybe they're planning something. Come up under the sand or cut them off. It wouldn't be the first..."

A cry burst from him, startling his companion.

"What the fuck?"

The other brushed him aside and peered through the scope. Below them, hundreds of yards ahead, a fireball raced to the sky. The craft lay in pieces, a rumble from the blast reaching them. A trail of sand between it and the dome rained to the ground.

The man peering through the scope mumbled. "How'd they wreck it like that?"

"Never seen that. Squids don't move that fast."

A second explosion rocked the Waypoint, their scouting post trembled – the stench of frying food mixed with the roar of distant thunder as sand rained around them.

"That's not a squid."

Screams accompanied the implosion of the dome wall. Debris cascaded inside the Waypoint, raining steel and concrete over the inhabitants. A cloud of sand billowed from outside.

Their screams were cut short–as the last chunks of dome struck the ground, most were already dead.

Some bodies stood wide-eyed for milliseconds, gashes erupting across their frames, blood and tissue spilling before they could process or respond. Others were decapitated, dismembered, limbs dropping or flung helter-skelter.

Minor disturbances in objects around the victims from tents to storage containers provided the only other evidence of the Hunter as it completed its butchery. Medical tents were slashed. Carts overturned. Bodies decorated the marketplaces, dropped in the middle of everyday actions.

Only the Trunes raised any resistance. Most were killed in their cages, unable to defend themselves. A few of the more powerful or clever escaped their prisons in the panic of imminent death. They were also bright enough not to engage the Hunter, dashing for the desert through the damaged opening.

Each was tracked down and slaughtered.

The Waypoint massacre ended in a manner of minutes. The speed and time distortion of the Hunter turned the normal work of such an assault into the blink of an eye.

An unnatural silence fell over the ruptured enclosure, and the far wall of the dome collapsed, blown outward. A giant transport loomed nearby, awaiting masses inside that would never approach. Stunned arrivals and their guides on the sandship blinked to watch the line of people approaching the vehicle fall like dominoes in a maroon mist.

Their execution followed before they could comprehend what was unfolding. The thing entered the vehicle, the craft rocking on its treads to the path of the carnage.

Stillness followed.

No cries for help. No sounds of suffering within or without. Corpses carpeted the inside of the dome, the space between it and the transport, and the vehicle's interior.

The Hunter shifted into a more normal pace and paused before the smoking dome. Bladed appendages extended and retracted as the parched air and searing radiation dried the pools of blood and remains littering the sands.

It vanished again, a series of explosions and impacts sounding around and inside the structure. One by one, the central industrial elements supporting life were destroyed. Air filtration, waste and water systems, solar panels and the electrical grid. The thing reduced the structure to ruins so that should some remnant of humanity survive the culling, there would be nowhere for them to seek shelter.

Moments later, sand rose like a ski wake from the battered Waypoint and raced past those entombed in the roller. The displacement withdrew toward the horizon and the setting sun, the broiling orb a half circle on the ground. The much smaller half circle of the Great Dome cowered, silhouetted inside the expansive flame.

Around the dome, mounds rose from the sands. Black tentacles emerged from the moving red hills. They approached the simmering carcasses.

12

PARITY MODEL

Norm looked the Trune over in the failing light of sunset and frowned at his missing limb. "Looks like *you're* back to health. Squid snack does wonders, I guess."

Sekvanta snorted at the hulking cyborg, blood and gobbets of flesh clinging to exposed fangs as she licked them. A deep hole beside them stank of water and worms. Fenn dribbled liquid from a canister into the mouth of Gomez.

"Your color is improved," said the Synth. "The wound is healing and your blood supply slowly replenishing."

"Squid tastes just like chicken," Gomez coughed. He cast a side eye to the Trune. "And thank the monster for sharing."

The Trune ignored him.

Norm fiddled with the fusion controls on his torso, the movements awkward with a single hand.

"Got the bugs out, robot?"

Fenn stood and examined the bulging core on the cyborg's back.

"Temporarily. You need parts. The radiation leak will return. Access to the Great Dome repository would be essential if it were not impossible. If you engage the field again, your tissues will die."

Norm nodded. "Well, so. I'd better make that fight count, huh?"

Fenn was silent, his eyes following the shadow of the dome behind them. They were past the shelter now, into the deep desert, a half day's flight to the Ark. The only question remaining was whether the Hunter still busied itself with the shelters and inhabitants. Or did it approach them now?

Norm followed the Synth's gaze and squinted.

"What the—"

He turned his eyes away as a blinding flash lit the sands. Tertiary lids dropped over the Trune's eyes, filtering the brilliance. Sekvanta stared along with Fenn at the gargantuan fireball rolling to the heavens.

The brilliance dimmed. Norm shielded his eyes, viewing forward.

"Mushroom cloud."

"The end of our long efforts here," said Fenn. "Our enemy triggered the fusion core. I assume the Waypoint is also destroyed."

Gomez closed his eye. "I guess you Synths win in the end."

"Arrivals still coming," mumbled Norm.

"Less frequently," said Fenn. "The rate is tapering off. My conservative models have two or three more centuries of arrivals with ever decreasing numbers. The tail end of the distribution. They will arrive to nothing. No shelter. No food. No knowledge of how to survive. Like the first waves, they will die. Horribly."

"Trunes also die," said Sekvanta. "Human Synth make Trunes. Put in cages. Hurt. Then send to die. Better all humans die."

Norm sighed. "Gotta say I'm having trouble with a counter-argument these days."

Gomez glared at Sekvanta. "You sound like team Hunter."

She returned the glare. "Hunter is *Synth*. Good too Synths die. Good Hunter dies."

"We need to fly again," said Fenn. "The Hunter has completed part of its mission. We are the last task. It is coming."

Norm scowled. "Can we even make the Ark?"

"I don't know. Estimating from the fastest I have measured, yes. However, I am skeptical we have observed its peak speed."

Gomez exhaled. "Jesus. What, then?"

"We need a distraction. Something to slow it, engage it, while we make a desperate run."

"Good luck distracting that mother-fucker," barked Norm. "Two domes in a day? Like roping a calf. I bet it didn't break a sweat."

"We must plan in the air," said Fenn.

The Trune lowered her wing. "Sekvanta ready to fly."

Without further words, the troop mounted the Trune, Gomez staggering, propped by Norm and Fenn. They laid him on the great back of the beast.

"A moment," said the Synth. "I will climb that large dune and scout. Perhaps I can locate the Hunter and estimate its velocity, produce a revised calculation."

"Will it matter?" asked Norm.

"Perhaps not. But information can sometimes play an essential role."

Fenn leapt off Sekvanta and dashed forward, soon lost in the night.

"Hell of a way for all this to end," said Gomez,

drinking in the brightening stars overhead. They twinkled over his faceplate and reflected from the lens of his eye.

"You know it. I always thought we'd just peter out after the arrivals ended. So few women, babies. Short lives. Or maybe another war. Or some planet-sized sandstorm wrecking the domes for good. Never imagined some super-killing machine from the past would show up and mow us all down."

"Not likely anyone's first thought."

Gears whirred as the cyborg turned his head toward Gomez. "You know we were always doomed."

"Yeah."

"Guess that thing's got a plan to finish it ahead of schedule."

"Synths are nothing but thorough. Programming's strong with them." Gomez laughed. "Programming's strong with us, too. Just sloppier."

Norm's face tightened, the skin taut between embedded elements of metal and plastic. He turned in the direction Fenn had left.

"Programming," he muttered. "What would you say Fenn's programming is all about?"

Gomez frowned, his half-face drooping.

"Fenn? I swear I don't know how those things think."

Sekvanta rumbled. "Fenn love humans. Love Trunes, too. Fenn protect. Fenn gone to Hunter."

"What?" asked Gomez. He leaned forward.

Norm sighed. "Yeah. That's what I was thinking."

"Wait. What do you mean?"

"Remember that *diversion* it was talking about? I think that stupid Synth's going to be the diversion."

"It's going to the Hunter?"

"Makes sense. We can't outrun it. We can't outfight it. Maybe Fenn thinks it can slow the thing down. Give us enough time to reach the Ark."

"It'll rip the bastard to pieces!"

"That's for sure. *Programming.* Self-sacrifice. For us. Should've realized." Norm turned to Sekvanta.

"Let's get airborne, honey. Don't want our friend to die for nothing."

13

LAST STANDING

Sekvanta landed before the yawning maw of the cave, the sun high overhead. Her passengers scrambled off, Gomez seeking shelter in her shade from the sun. Norm lumbered forward, pausing in front of the Trune and scrutinizing the darkness of the cavern.

"So this is it?" said Gomez, the glass eyes of his suit peering out from under the shadow of Sekvanta's wings.

"Suppose so. Told you, never been here myself."

The ground trembled, a heavy clanking accompanying the vibrations. Norm turned to Gomez.

"We got company."

Emerging from the shadows inside, a metal giant lumbered toward them. Obscene rotor canons and missile launchers protruded from each limb and the chassis was covered in thick battle armor. Smoke rose from the left shoulder of the mech, the armor wrecked. A small figure could be made out through a glass window atop the warbot.

Sekvanta growled and tensed, but eased her stance as she observed the thing. Sensing danger, Gomez braved the light and limped beside Norm, propping himself on the cyborg's metal shoulder pads.

"What the hell is that?"

"The Woman," said Norm. His face was tight.

The mech approached them, and the Trune in particular, stopping meters away from Sekvanta. The beast glared into the cockpit, her golden eyes boring into the white scars of the pilot. The pair remained motionless, only the sound of the shifting sand and wind disturbing the moment. The mech reached out a powerful arm toward the creature.

Sekvanta did not recoil, but arched her neck toward the hand. The mechanical giant stroked the back of her head. A voice of static burst from speakers in the mech.

"You have such beautiful light."

Norm coughed. "Not to interrupt, but, we're kinda in a hurry. Got hell's posse on our asses."

The hand retracted and the woman glanced across them. Cyborg, human, and Trune.

"Where is Fenn?"

"We don't know," said Norm, his voice low. "Damn fool ran out to meet the Hunter. Didn't tell us. Think it wanted to slow it down. Buy us some time to get here. Thank God we made it."

"Fenn failed." Her voice cracked. "And you're too late."

The two humanoid figures gawked at each other and turned to the mech.

"What do you mean?" asked Norm.

Sekvanta rumbled. "Trunes cried. Death inside. Hunter here."

Answering her proclamation, a rush of air shook them all, Gomez losing his balance and falling to the ground. Sekvanta spun in place like a mountainous cat. Her claws extended as her feet slapped the sand, teeth bared and a growl slipping her lips.

Norm pivoted without haste, all too sure what he would see.

Behind them, the nightmare loomed without sound. Its countless limbs were still, the blades red and dripping. Impaled on each was a Trune. Some small, some enormous. All were dead.

The Hunter slung the bodies to the ground, the

impacts thunderous and wet. The mech marched forward as the woman surveyed the slaughter with her blind eyes.

"Even the Angel," she said toward the broken carcass of a giant Trune with wings. She pivoted to Sekvanta, placing a metal hand on the Trune's broad back. "What hope can there be now?"

Delivering a punishing blow, the Hunter cast a tentacle forward. Pieces of a body thudded to the ground. White hair and pale skin protruded from a multicolored goo coating the mangled remains.

"Fenn," said the Woman.

A rumbling hum jumped in pitch as the cyborg blinked and phase-shifted, his frame a blurred and skipping image.

"Sorry, amigo. You deserved better. But we'll give this bastard all we have."

Norm and the Trune vanished before the eyes of Gomez and the Woman. The Hunter stuttered in and out of vision, never changing its position, yet always seeming to move. The deadly appendages were a blur as it casually parried the coordinated attack. Blasts of displaced air swept over the powerless pair as the sound barrier was shattered again and again.

Blood sprayed. Fragments of metal and flesh were flung every which way. Human screams and the cries of monsters shot like rockets through the mayhem.

The body of Norm was ejected from the melee. Cut in half from belly to brain, wiring and flesh bursting ribald, his ruined corpse landed twitching mere feet from the stunned observers.

The Trune roared and yelped as a wing fragment hurled skyward, her severed tail slamming against the side of the cavern entrance. Sekvanta crashed to the earth, crawling away from the Hunter, a tentacle launching skyward and crashing down. It speared her through the skull, blood and brains exploding like a dropped melon.

"No," whispered the Woman.

Another lanced Gomez through the chest, lifting him above the mech. He was diced into ribbons and a crimson mist that rained on the window of the cockpit.

The Woman opened fire at the shimmering apparition. She launched all her missiles and unloaded the complete contents of the hulking cannons at her sides.

She hit nothing.

The Hunter solidified in her vision, displaced a hundred yards to reform mere inches from her mech. Behind it the rockets exploded harmlessly into the dunes.

"God damn you."

The tentacles sang as they blurred, the mech dissected, oils and wiring spilling like burst blood vessels. The chassis split and teetered, and she tumbled.

The impact knocked the breath from her, and she gasped on all fours, spitting sand from her mouth. The towering presence of the killer pressed down on her like death.

Her joints popped. She pushed her frail body up, legs atrophied and shaking, glaring forward with egg-white eyes to the towering horror.

"What are you waiting for, demon?"

A bladed limb arced over her head. A rush of energy poured through her. Time slowed, the deadly appendage hanging impossibly long in the sky. Once limited to visions of light, she could now see. Each razored protuberance clarified to infinite detail, the glints of the red giant showering beams over her and the ground.

Her death blow fell as through molasses. Her

muscles tensed, the thousand scalpels nearing, the mass of the arm an approaching battering ram set to shatter her weak bones.

She screamed.

14

BEAUTIFUL LIGHT

The Hunter's arm exploded.

The Woman sensed only the slightest of touches, a feather sliding against the side of her body. She gaped in wonder as the tentacle burst into fragments at her side. A thousand shards of metal and unknown elements scattered over and around her.

The hulking colossus slunk backward. Not in an eye blink, devoid of the shimmering time-distortion. At a dream's pace under the power of its many limbs.

She examined the unscathed arm and extended her hands, palms up. Her long creviced skin was unwrinkled, unburned, lustrous with the tone and hue of youth.

What's happening?

Did it matter? In the madness of this hateful sun,

standing around the broken bodies that mocked her long hope, explanations meant nothing.

Only vengeance.

Forgoing sanity, the Woman leapt forward and attacked the synthetic demogorgon. Once-wobbly legs powered her forward and she rocketed toward the retreating Synth. The thing aimed strikes, most too slow. But several neared her darting torso. She cut through them like spiderwebs, the once impenetrable extremities of the Hunter turned to glass shards to rain over the sands.

She landed on the bulk of the Hunter, its surface morphing underneath into blades and new arms. The Woman raised a fist above her and bellowed as she brought it down like a hammer.

The skin of the Synth split, internal components splattering from a titanic impact. Deeper she drove her arm, until she had buried it to her shoulder in the bowels of the thing. A hunger and instinct pulled her hand, guiding it, leading her fingers inward.

She touched a crystalline core at the center. Wrapping her hand around it, she yanked a glowing orb into the light of the sun. Semi-organic parts and wires clung to it and dangled along her arm.

The Hunter shuddered, the limbs drooping to its sides. Small, creeping spaghetti poured from the rend in its side and climbed toward the orb. The extending worms wrapped around her body and arm, seeking the sphere she held high. It burned red in the star's radiance.

She squeezed. Words escaped the entity under her.

"Stop."

She did not. Hairline cracks appeared in the sides of the orb. The filigree strands raced up her arm, grasping her hand, frantic to pry the ball out of her palm.

But they could not. Tighter and harder she contracted. The small fissures widened. The sentient gemstone split, and with a final cry the orb imploded in her fleshly vice.

Still she crushed. The large shards fractured further, until small diamonds trickled through her fingers and pelleted the red sand below.

The Hunter's arms dropped to the desert floor. The microsnakes sagged and the Woman reached up and ripped them from her arm. She turned her palm up, diamond dust coating it, and glowered at the thing of malice beneath her.

She wept.

I WILL BE WITH YOU ALWAYS.

EVEN UNTIL THE END OF THIS AGE.

"No!"

Her cry tore through her throat. She pounded the surface of the dead Hunter, the impacts bloodying her hand.

"Come down, daughter. Your quest awaits."

The Woman turned around. A shadow shimmered amidst the mauled bodies and wreckage. Yet not a shadow. The apparition was a hallucinogen of smoke made flesh, never still, never settling on a single manifestation. Humanoid and so sized. It spoke with a genderless inflection.

"Come down, I say, and leave that foul thing."

She floated. Her feet left the Hunter's surface and her body drifted away over the sands. She descended, brushing the sands only feet from the shadow man.

"I can see," she whispered. Brown eyes burned down at her palms. "My body...is new. And I stopped it. *Impossible.* Everything impossible."

"Nothing is impossible to those who believe."

The Woman scanned the shadow.

"What are you?"

"I'm the incarnate deus ex machina. I am salvation."

She dropped to her knees, wrapping her arms around her body. She shook with sobs.

"Salvation? You're too late, *savior*. Everything is lost. Why did you ever bring me out of that desert? Lie to me with that voice and beautiful light? Why give us hope when it would end this way?"

"Ye of little faith."

"Faith!" Her cry echoed in the nearby cave. "Faith? In what, now? Look around, Godthing. They're all dead! All the Trunes. All the people on this fucking awful hellhole. The ship is destroyed! There's not a goddamned thing left!"

Tears dripped from her eyes and she placed her head in her hands. "Faith. What the hell am I supposed to have faith in now?" Her shoulders shook.

Water?

The Woman raised her nascent eyes. Rapids churned in the space around them.

"Be at peace, daughter."

Gray clouds melted from the fingers of the apparition, a swarm of nanolocusts buzzing in a whispered frenzy, branching and streaming in multiple directions. Undiminished by the river of material bleeding outward, the entity echoed an icon, arms outstretched, dark clouds forming around the mangled forms of the slain creatures, alighting on their surfaces.

She gasped. The murky fog penetrated the corpses, entering each orifice, worming through skin and wounds.

The flesh twitched.

"What's happening?"

"Believe, and you shall see."

Hard Time, Book 6: Deity

In Book 6, **Deity,** an entity guides a motley crew of creatures toward a new beginning in a planet's last gasp at life.

www.ingramcontent.com/pod-product-compliance
Lightning Source LLC
Chambersburg PA
CBHW020634130626
46552CB00003B/1218